BRUNO HÄCHLER grew up in the Zürcher Oberland, the hilly region outside of Zurich, Switzerland. He has worked as a typesetter, a newspaper editor, and a music journalist. In Bruno Hächler's songs and stories, mischief and poetry go hand in hand. Hächler has written numerous children's books that have been translated into many different languages. He has also put out a slew of albums of children's music, many of which have reached the Swiss charts. His album "Langi Ohre" was selected by an all-child jury to receive the Lollipop Award for best children's album. Today Hächler is a full-time writer of children's songs and children's books. He lives in Winterthur, Switzerland. www.brunohaechler.ch

LAURA D'ARCANGELO was born in Bern, Switzerland, and grew up in Ins, a small village in Seeland that is the birthplace of the painter Albert Anker. In 2017 she completed her studies in illustration fiction at the Lucerne University of Applied Sciences and Arts (Hochschule Luzern). Since then she has worked as a freelance illustrator and as an author and illustrator of children's books. Currently she is completing a master's program in teaching art so that she can soon start working as an art educator. But what she likes most of all is to take gouache and colored pencils and create little worlds on the page. She has published two previous picture books that have both been nominated for several prizes. www.lauradarcangelo.ch

TO MAMI AND PAPI, MAM AND PA, NONNA AND NONNO,
WHO WOULD ALSO CARRY ME ON THEIR BACKS TO
THE END OF THE WORLD – L. D'A.

BRUNO HÄCHLER

LAURA D'ARCANGELO

ROOM ON TOP

TRANSLATED BY MARSHALL YARBROUGH

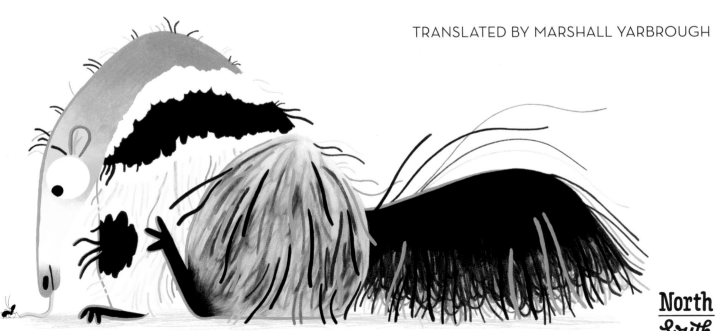

NorthSouth

The little anteater rocked back and forth as he rode around on his mother's back.

It was just the best, sitting on Mama's back.

Looking around. Loving life.

Only he did feel a bit lonely sometimes. . . .

"Hello, Badger!" cried the little anteater.
"Wanna go for a ride?"

MEEEP
MEEEP!

The badger looked a lot like the little anteater.
All except for the nose, that is.

"Be glad to," he politely replied—
he had nothing better to do.
He climbed up on Mama's back
and looked around.

"How bright!" he said excitedly.

Compared to Mama's back, his burrow was rather musty and dark.

"Hello, Duck!" cried the little anteater.
"Wanna go for a ride?"

— MEEEEP?

The duck didn't need
to be asked twice.

QUA-WA-WA-WACK

"How roomy!" he quacked...

and thought of the cramped nest where the ducklings lived with their mother.

"Hello, Hare!" cried the little anteater.
"Wanna go for a ride?"

— WHOOOOOOSHH

Did he ever! The hare snuggled
up in between the duck, the badger,
and the little anteater.

"How stylish!" he said.
He was talking about Mama's black stripes.

A squirrel hopped down from her branch—and landed right on the badger's head.

"How cozy!" she squeaked.

Her nest was way up high and no place for the faint of heart.

The frog brought his
whole family along.

"How dry!" he croaked.

RRRIBBITT!

RIBBITT!

OOOPH

In his pond, everyone went to bed with wet feet every night.

There was quite a crowd
on Mama's back by now.
A real tower.

HOOPF!

But the little anteater
kept making new friends.

"How fast," said the snail.　　　　　　"How practical," said the fox.

_OOOOOH

FNNRRROOO!
FNNRRROOFF!

"How comfortable," said the woodpecker.
"How airy," said the mole.

"I wanna come too,"
said the dormouse.

With every gust of wind the tower teetered dangerously back and forth.

Just then a heron with long,
thin legs perched on the tip of the tower.

"How wobbly!" he squawked.
And then . . .

Dormouse
Mole
Woodpecker
Fox
Snail
Frog and family too
Squirrel
Hare
Duck
and Badger
all went tumbling headfirst
onto the grass.

But the little anteater
still sat in his spot
on Mama's back.

And as he rode around,
rocking back and forth,

he thought how there was
no better place in the world.

For little anteaters,
at least . . .

Copyright © 2022 by NordSüd Verlag AG, CH-8050 Zürich, Switzerland.
First published in Switzerland under the title "Noch Einer Oben Drauf"
English translation copyright © 2022 by NorthSouth Books, Inc.,
New York 10016.
Translated by Marshall Yarbrough

First published in the United States, Great Britain, Canada, Australia,
and New Zealand in 2022 by NorthSouth Books, Inc., an imprint of
NordSüd Verlag AG, CH-8050 Zürich, Switzerland.

Distributed in the United States by NorthSouth Books, Inc.,
New York 10016.
Library of Congress Cataloging-in-Publication Data is available.
ISBN: 978-0-7358-4486-5 (trade edition)
1 3 5 7 9 · 10 8 6 4 2
Printed in Latvia by Livonia Print, Riga, 2022.
www.northsouth.com

Climate neutral
Print product
ClimatePartner.com/17658-2110-1001